A LITTLE SPOT

ABC's of PEACEFUL

DIANE ALBER

To my children, Ryan and Anna.

This book belongs to:

_____

_____

_____

A Peaceful Spot is in us all,
It may be big or it may be small.

Here are ways to be PEACEFUL every day,
and learn your letters along the way!

A

Is for **ANIMALS** that give lots of cuddles when you need a break.

B is for **BLOWING BUBBLES**.
Now take a deep breath.

C

is for COUNTING. How many SPOTS do you see?

D is for **DRAWING** your Peaceful SPOT.

E is for **EXERCISE**. A short walk can be just what you need.

F is for **FINDING** things that are round.

G is for GIGGLES. Can you tell a funny story or joke?

H

is for **H**UGGING someone who cares about you.

I

is for **IMAGINING** a peaceful place.

J

is for **JUMPING** all your sillies out!

K is for **KITE** flying on a beautiful day.

L is for **LISTENING** to a bedtime story.

M

is for MUSIC that helps you relax.

N is for **NAPPING** in a cozy place.

O is for **OUTDOOR** play in fresh air.

P is for fun **PUZZLES** .

Q

**is for QUIETLY reading
a good book.**

R is for a **RAINBOW** hunt. Try and find something of every color of the rainbow.

S is for **SINGING** your favorite song.

T

is for a **TEA** party with friends.

U is for **USING** this time to be peaceful.

V

is for **VEGETABLES**. Is it time for a healthy snack?

W is for **WATERCOLOR** painting.

X

is for **X**YLOFOX. Make up a fun word. This one is a fox playing a xylophone.

Y  is for **YOGA**. What is your favorite pose?

Z is for a **ZEN** garden. Make a garden with sand and stones.

From the Author:

Thank you for reading this book! I had a huge request to make beginner books that would be a great introduction to the spot series for little learners, so I created several books to do just that. Now, not only can children learn their letters and numbers, but they can learn how to name their feelings too! Big emotions can be overwhelming for small ones, and learning to name them can be tricky. This book aims to make it fun and engaging at the same time.

Diane Alber

Made in United States
North Haven, CT
21 June 2023

38043607R00020